FROZEN *Promises*

A HOLIDAY BILLIONAIRE ROMANCE

ANASTASIA DEAN

For those who like a dash of drama with their spicy Christmas books.

AUTHOR'S NOTE

This book contains elements of:

- Marriage separation
- Unhappiness in marriage
- Explicit sexual scenes

Please make sure you are protecting your mental health. If you need more information, send me a message on any of my socials. Otherwise, happy reading!

CHAPTER 1

'TIS THE SEASON FOR LETDOWNS

Catalina

I have no business cooking, yet my kitchen smells like a gingerbread man's asshole after a long day of eating peppermint patties. I'm no chef, but it's basically Santa's Workshop here, and I'm the sexy, chubby elf giving all the other elves something to drool over. The red Santa apron tied around my waist does little to protect the tiny, green velvet dress hiding underneath. I'm dressed for aesthetic, not practicality.

I'm attempting to film my annual Christmas Cookie baking video. Santiago, my best friend and personal assistant, centers the camera on the tripod, giving me a thumbs up once I'm in frame. "Wait, where's your Santa hat? Didn't you buy a Santa hat?"

I probably did. It's probably stored away somewhere in my beauty room, collecting dust. While I was shopping yesterday, I found the cutest headband with a sparkly red and green elf hat with a giant pom-pom sewed to the top. I bought two, one for me and one for Elias . . . who is ten minutes late.

He's going to show up.

He promised.

The small, nagging voice in the back of my mind reminds me he's made promises before that he broke. Foolishly, I get my hopes up each time, hoping he'd put me before his work for once. He used to put me first, and I think he will again. If he doesn't...no. I'm not going there yet.

Instead, I focus on the two red bowls of icing sitting on my island. Icing sugar cookies is a two-person job for this video.

Santiago gestures to his watch, noting the time. "Should we call him?" His voice is soft and gentle, like he's carefully navigating a minefield. One wrong step and I'll combust.

"I'm sure he'll be here in ten minutes," I say, feigning more confidence than I feel. I'm a natural at putting on an appearance in front of the camera. As a plus-size blogger that shares parts of her life, I've embraced the person my social media followers want me to be. It's not fake exactly . . .just a caricature of my true self that I don when filming.

Santiago raises a sculpted brow, knowing I'm full of shit. "Do you want me to step in? People love your gay best friend."

I groan. "I swear I'm trying to get them to call you by your name."

Santiago just waves me off. "I don't care, boo. Most of them are all in good nature. Why don't we record, and if Elias comes home, he can jump in?"

It's not a bad idea, so I nod. "Are you camera ready?"

"Girl please, I'm always camera ready. Give me some spiked eggnog, and I'm good to go."

"We don't have eggnog."

"Ugh, fine," he sighs dramatically and clicks on the camera. The red light turns on, signaling it's recording. Santiago will edit out all the unnecessary shit people don't want to see. The man is a genius at editing, making my videos look more professional than I could ever achieve. Since I've hired him, their quality has improved, and I've gained nearly a million followers. It is crazy to think about a million people watching me, Catalina Ayala, a chubby girl from Texas sharing part of her soul. It's one of the only places I feel like I can express myself, especially with Elias busy all the time.

Santiago rounds the island, giving me a thumbs up. I plaster the biggest smile on my face, looking directly into the camera. "Hey beautiful people," I say with practiced enthusiasm, my lips curving in a rehearsed smile. Behind me, the Christmas tree atop my counter glows gold and green, creating a perfectly festive backdrop. "Today, we're decorating sugar cookies and spilling a little holiday tea, so grab your cocoa and let's hang out."

I slip effortlessly into my groove, performing for the camera as if it's second nature, because it is. Unlike the messy unpredictability of my personal life, my online persona offers a welcome escape—a carefully curated world where I'm in control. Vlogging isn't just a job; it's a passion that I've turned into a thriving career.

My Christmas vlogs always draw a big audience, and with Santiago by my side, I know this one will be no exception. Our chemistry is effortless, an unspoken rhythm that makes every interaction feel natural. We feed off each other's energy, turning even the simplest moments into something engaging and worth watching.

Admittedly, our cookie decorating sucks, and we will never be the next Martha Stewart or be hired as Ho-Ho-Ho Elves at Santa's Pub. The candy cane I attempted decorating looks more like a bloody fish hook, and Santiago's snowman looks like a bubble wand curler. They taste hella good though, so we didn't completely fuck them up.

"The recipe and all the utensils we used today will be linked in the description below with my affiliate code to get 15 percent off. I'll be back after Christmas with a huge giveaway, so make sure you are on the lookout. Bye sexy babes, and make good choices." I wave at the camera, blowing a kiss before taking another bite of my cookie.

"And that's a wrap!" Santiago grins, hurrying behind the camera to turn it off. "I'll get this edited tonight, so we can upload it tomorrow. Sound good?"

"Yes, thank you. And thank you for stepping in." I glance at the time on the oven and frown. Elias was supposed to be home an hour ago. Did he get held up in a meeting with a client? Part of me wonders if he's chatting up one of the pretty secretaries at work. Elias is many things, but a cheater isn't one of them. I only know that because of the way he ripped his cousin a new asshole after finding out he cheated on his pregnant girlfriend.

Still, the thought lingers.

"Feel free to use my computer to edit. I'm going to call Elias quickly."

"No problem. Is it cool if Noah comes over? I told him I'd be working late, and he wanted to have dinner with me while I worked."

I smile. Noah, Santiago's husband, is one of the sweetest people I've ever met and perfect for my best friend. "Of course. I'm going to step outside and make the call."

Santiago smiles sympathetically at me and nods. "Okay, feel free to join us when you're done."

I nod absentmindedly and step outside onto our covered patio. The cool evening air brushes against my skin as I fish my phone from my pocket. With a sigh, I sink into the plush cushions of the outdoor couch and dial Elias.

The phone rings once . . . .twice . . . each unanswered ring stretches the silence, tightening the knot of anticipation in my stomach. It would be typical of him not to answer. As I begin to think he won't pick up, the call connects on the final ring.

"Catalina," Elias says. His voice is muffled, like he's driving with his windows down.

"Where are you?"

"On my way home. I got held up at the office," he says. I've heard this excuse a thousand times before. He always gets held up at the office. Forget 9 a.m.-5 p.m.; he's there from the ass crack of dawn to late into the night. Week-days, weekends. He's never home. It's like our house is the plague, and he stays far away from it. But here I am, sitting alone in our 6,400-square-foot mansion every night. Everything reminds me of him and the life we built together, but he's not here to share it with me.

We used to spend every waking hour together. Our hands couldn't stop roaming each other's body, and kisses lasted way into the night. My heart lurches, thinking of everything I miss so desperately in our marriage.

"You missed filming today." My words are greeted with silence.

Elias curses. "Fuck, cariño. That was tonight?"

The question makes me grit my teeth. This man who meticulously schedules everything into his calendar, who would literally rather get run over by a semi-truck than miss a meeting with a client, conveniently forgot about our plans. It's like a dagger to my heart.

"Yeah, it was, *cariño*," I snarl, unable to keep the vehemence out of my tone with the term of endearment. "Next time I'll call your secretary and have her schedule me a meeting. Maybe then you'll remember."

"Catalina—"

"Don't 'Catalina' me!" I realize I'm yelling when the neighbor's dog starts barking as if defending his home from intruders. "I'm so tired of this, Elias! When are you going to show up for me?"

"Show up for you?" Bitter laughter barrels through the phone and grates my nerves. "You think because I'm not standing right next to you, I'm not showing up? I'm out here handling things—*real* things that need me and keep everything else running so you can breathe easy at night. This isn't about not caring. It's about priorities and responsibilities. Shit doesn't stop because the holidays are coming."

A whirlwind of thoughts blows through my mind, begging to be screamed. But just as quickly, the fight drains from me. I'm exhausted from this endless cycle, from always battling for a sliver of his attention. My throat tightens, and I bite down on the urge to speak because I know if I open my mouth, a sob might slip out. I refuse to cry for him. I'm too damn angry for tears.

Silence stretches between us. I'm tempted to hang up and ignore him, but his next words catch me off guard.

"Let me make it up to you. Dinner tomorrow? We can go to that steakhouse you like?"

Hope flickers to life, fragile yet persistent, amid the storm raging inside me. It's dangerous, probably reckless, but I cling to it because it's the only thing keeping me afloat. He did this the last time we argued; he promised me a date, but ended up having a work thing come up. Still, I want to believe this time will be different. I need to believe it. "I would like that." My voice is softer than I intend, laced with uncertainty for our future.

One dinner won't mend the cracks in our foundation, but it might be a start. It's a sign he's willing to try, he sees and hears me, and he wants to fight for us as much as I do. Because I can't keep holding our relationship together on my own. He needs to prove he wants this.

If nothing changes, if he lets this slip through his fingers, I know the truth I've been too afraid to say aloud: our marriage is beyond repair.

And I'm not sure I have the strength to keep treading water much longer.

CHAPTER 2

CALENDAR FULL, MARRIAGE EMPTY

Elias

I expect Catalina to be awake, pacing around the foyer, ready to read my ass to filth, when I get home. Some of it is warranted, but my wife doesn't see the big picture like I do. Every damn thing I do is for us.

When I walk in, light radiates from the Christmas trees sporadically placed throughout the house—Catalina's doing, not mine.

Light comes from Catalina's office, but when I peak in, I only see her assistant, Santiago. The man is here at all strange hours, editing whatever video Catalina filmed that day. He's so submerged in his work that he doesn't notice me staring. I duck out a moment later.

I find my wife in our bed, sprawled out on her side. She's in that satin camisole and shorts set I bought her for her birthday. I can make out her curves, the same curves I think about every fucking day before I go to work. If there's one thing I regret, it's not fucking my wife as much as she deserves. A woman like that drives a man feral.

I take my time removing my suit, piece by piece, letting them fall to the floor for the housekeepers to deal with later. As far as I'm concerned, my girl shouldn't have to lift a damn finger—not if I can help it.

I slide into bed beside her, careful not to wake her. Catalina lets out a soft groan and shifts onto her side, turning away from me before settling back into sleep. Her presence is agony—a sweet, addictive kind of torment I can't get enough of.

I fall asleep to the soft sound of her breathing.

But sleep doesn't last long. My body is jolted awake when my alarm goes off a few hours later, the sound reverberates around the quiet room. When I reach to turn it off, a soft, feminine hand brushes my shoulder.

"Dinner tonight," Catalina whispers, still half asleep.

My day is packed, starting with the gym, a final hearing with a client who's been a pain since day one, and then to the office for meetings. Somehow, I have to fit dinner in. "I'll meet you tonight." The words, which I hope aren't lies, fall off my lips easily. "Go back to sleep, cariño. I'll see you tonight."

Satisfied with my answer, Catalina lets out a soft sigh and withdraws her hand, turning away from me as she snuggles back under the covers. She pulls the blanket up to her chin, tucking herself into its warmth. Within moments, her breathing evens out, and she's asleep again —peaceful and undisturbed.

I'm left lying there, awake and alone with my thoughts. The familiar stillness of the room marks the beginning of another day. Just like every morning.

I HADN'T BEEN SURPRISED to find another NFL player waiting in my office after my afternoon meetings. He fits my clientele, which includes professional sports players, A-list celebrities, and politicians who find themselves in the midst of another scandal. They call me to clear their names that have been dragged through the dirt.

And I always do. For a pretty penny, that is.

The man stands, patting down his already pristine suit. He offers me his hand, which I take. Strong grip. Something I can appreciate.

"Mr. Ayala, it's a pleasure to meet you." Even as he says it, his shoulders stiffen and his lips purse in a tight line. It's clear he doesn't want to be here. No one wants to end up in legal trouble.

"And your name?" I ask.

The man furrows his brows, pursed lips turning into a frown. These big shots hate when I don't automatically recognize their faces, but how could I? I spend every waking hour at my job. If I'm not meeting with clients, I'm working with my managing partner, César Estrada. He's the closest thing I have to a brother. We were two broke kids who built our empire from the ground up with our blood, sweat, and tears. It paid off.

"My name is Joaquin Cortez, and this is my manager, Leon Travers." Joaquin steps aside. and for the first time since entering my office, I notice the smaller man. He's in a fine, luxurious, and unmistakably expensive suit similar to Joaquin's. The kind of suit that proclaims they can afford my specific expertise and time.

Leon shakes my hand, stepping past Joaquin. "Gotta

admit, Mr. Ayala, I didn't think I'd get face time with you anytime soon."

"Yes, well, my client list is ever growing—"

Leon shakes his head, cutting me off, which I loathe. "Nah, man. Because it's the holidays, getting anyone on the phone this month has been a fucking headache." He gestures back toward Joaquin. "And this guy has already given me enough damn headaches to last a lifetime. I'm five years sober, man, but I swear his goal is to drive me back to the bottle."

"So fucking dramatic," Joaquin says, rolling his eyes with a scoff, barely bothering to look up.

"No, I fucking ain't," Leon snaps back. The contention between them nearly smothers me. I rarely, if ever, get managers coming in with their clients, so whatever Joaquin did—or didn't do—is going to be one hell of a fight. Thankfully, that's my specialty. Hell, it's the specialty of the entire damn firm.

"See, man, we need your help. Joaquin is my best client—"

"He means I make his ass the most money," Joaquin grumbles before sinking back into his seat, a haughty expression on his face. He holds his tension in his shoulders. Though he's attempting to prove he's calm and collected, the cracks in his armor tell me otherwise.

"Take a seat, Mr. Travers, and we can get started," I say, gesturing toward the empty chair.

Leon gives a curt nod before lowering himself back into the seat. As he settles in, I turn toward my desk, ready to begin, until the sudden chime of my phone interrupts me. I pause. A pang of annoyance flickers through me as I reach into my pocket, realizing I'd forgotten to silence it this morning. I pull the device out, and the screen lights up with a new notification.

I frown.

It's from my wife.

> The driver is taking me to dinner. I'll meet you there.

Fuck.

This morning's conversation comes back, reminding me of the promise I made to Catalina. I had made the reservations last night without knowing I'd get this last-minute meeting. I glance at the time on my phone. It's a quarter till six o'clock. Fifteen minutes won't hurt, and then I can head to dinner. Looks like I will be spending the rest of my night in my home office, though.

"You have fifteen minutes. Start from the beginning and tell me why you're here."

I nudge my mouse, waking my computer from sleep. With a few quick clicks my notes pull up, ready to capture every detail of their story. I focus in, giving Leon and Joaquin my full attention. They're my clients, and they know I'm in their corner—always. I advocate fiercely, no matter what's happening in my life. Even when things are messy behind the scenes, my clients get my best. I can't have it any other way.

Leon carries most of the conversation, his voice steady and assured, while Joaquin chimes in with brief remarks. Their words hold no surprises for me. I've heard it all before. Years of working with A-list clients has exposed me to every possible crisis and every desperate plea for solutions. It takes a lot to shock me. But for them, every problem feels like a ticking time bomb, a looming disaster threatening to unravel everything they've built. To them,

I'm not just an advisor. I'm their last line of defense against losing it all.

Leon starts detailing the chaos Joaquin has managed to land himself in. It's a full-blown scandal: a DUI, illegal possession of a firearm, a defamation claim that's gaining traction, and a very public meltdown making its rounds online. This kind of mess that will take more than legal skill. It'll take a miracle to clean up. But I've worked harder cases and won.

As Leon speaks, my phone chimes again. I glance down, momentarily pulled from the wreckage he's laying out.

> Here. Where are you?

Then a second later.

> You haven't even left your office, have you?! Elias, what the actual fuck?

I curse silently, stuck between wanting to stay but knowing I needed to go. Leon, clearly oblivious to my dilemma, drones on, but I put my hand up, stopping him mid-sentence. "Listen, I have enough to get started. I'll contact you both as well as our PR agency soon. They're experts at rebuilding public images. In the meantime, I advise keeping a low profile."

Leon snorts, which earns him a hard jab to the shoulder from Joaquin. I stand, reaching out my hand to shake theirs as they stand. "I'll be in touch." Then I grab my business card from inside my jacket pocket and hand one to each of them. "Call me if anything changes."

That should have been the end of it. Hell, I tried ending this meeting and wrapping this shit up, but it took another ten minutes to get Leon and Joaquin out of my office. By then Catalina is blowing up my phone. I leave my office in a pissy mood. I don't like being rushed. Catalina knows this. She knows the dedication I put into my work for us to have the lifestyle we have. It should excuse me being a few minutes late to a damn dinner.

Since the universe is determined to piss me off, I hit every fucking light from my office to the restaurant downtown. By the time I pull up to valet, my nerves are shot, and I chuck the keys at the poor attendant, hitting him perhaps a little too hard in the chest. I'll tip him well after I meet my wife, who is still blowing up my phone.

The hostess with the fake smile greets me when I walk in, but I skip the pleasantries and have her lead me to where Catalina is. I half expect my wife not to be there. I'm twenty minutes late, so I can't blame her if she left. It will take a lot to get back in her good graces. The thought fills me with dread especially since I feel a weird barrier between us these days. It feels like she's shutting me out.

When we reach the table, Catalina is still there, her presence impossible to ignore. She's draped in a short, sequined dress that shimmers like the night sky on a clear evening, deep blue with flecks of silver that catch the light. The fabric clings to every curve of her soft, alluring body, making it nearly impossible to look away. I'm not the only one that thinks so because I catch a few men taking her in. It makes me murderous. She is, without a doubt, a goddess, breathtaking and untouchable. But this goddess is furious with her rage directed at me.

She doesn't greet me when I take a seat, only looks at me with narrowed eyes and tight lips. Her freshly manicured nails tap against the rim of her wine glass, and she's angled away from me, like she's ready to bolt.

Before I have a chance to say anything, a server comes by taking my drink order. From the corner of my eye, I notice Catalina's phone buzzing, which isn't unusual since her job revolves around social media. However, the way she glances at me before looking down and typing has my hackles rising.

When Catalina is done furiously texting, she puts her phone facedown on the table. She's hiding something from me.

"You know," she starts, speaking for the first time since I've gotten here, "I thought that maybe because you planned this, you'd actually arrive on time."

"I was held up—"

"In the office, I'm aware," she snaps. "That seems to be your excuse every time. So, I've been thinking, you haven't sent me your schedule for a long time. So, I went into your office today—"

"You went into my office?" She knows I hate people in my home office without permission. My eyes narrow. I keep a few things to myself, and my office is one of them. Not because I'm hiding anything from Catalina, but because there is confidential information in there. I have things on my desk I don't want touched or seen.

"And I logged into your work computer," she continues as if I haven't even spoken, "because I wanted to see your calendar. I thought surely my husband is working all these hours because he plans to take Christmas and New Year's off. And you know what I found?"

I know exactly what she found. My jaw clenches as I fight to keep my anger in check. I've never been good at controlling my temper, but Catalina is one of the few people I refuse to raise my voice at. She's my wife—she deserves my respect. Still, the bitterness rising in my throat is a sharp, acrid taste I can't swallow down.

"I'm doing this for us," I say, my voice steady but strained.

"For us?" She laughs humorlessly. "So, working during the holidays is for us? Working while I spend Christmas and New Year's alone is for us?"

"Yes, cariño. I do this to take care of us and to make sure we don't go without."

"But I'm going without you, Elias. Don't you see that?" she snaps back.

Anger boils over, and I can't hold back my frustration. "If you want to keep doing your silly little videos and traveling, then you're going to have to get used to me being gone or busy. This is the life you signed up for when you agreed to marry me."

The moment the words leave my lips, regret hits me like a freight train. A sharp ache twists in my gut as hurt, anger, and sadness flicker across Catalina's face. Each emotion lands a well-aimed punch. Her eyes glisten with unshed tears, but she blinks rapidly to hold them back.

"My *silly* videos?" she repeats, her voice quiet but sharp enough to make me flinch.

They aren't silly. I know. I've always known that.

But frustration had taken over. And instead of handling it like a rational person, I lashed out, letting the worst version of myself talk.

Fuck.

This isn't what I want.

"Cariño." I attempt to reach for her hand, but she yanks it away. I watch in horror as she pushes her chair back and stands. Her dress rides up her thigh. I shouldn't be focusing on that, but I do until she speaks again.

"I want to go home."

"Catalina—"

"Take me home, Elias. *Now*."

Catalina doesn't wait for a response. She turns sharply on her heel and strides toward the entrance, her back rigid with anger. She's walking away from me—away from this mess, leaving a suffocating weight behind.

I exhale slowly, forcing myself to believe that by morning, I'll find a way to fix this. I fix everyone else's shit, so I should be able to repair what's broken between us. She just needs time to cool off. We both do.

Sliding a few bills onto the table, I push back my chair and follow her outside. The night air is thick with tension, and I brace myself for the long, silent car ride home.

CHAPTER 3

SPACE FOR THE HOLIDAYS

Catalina

The air holds a bitter chill, matching the ice storm warring inside of me. I didn't want excuses tonight. I wanted commitment to us. Not his work. But all I got was the same damn excuses he always gives me. And then he called my videos *silly*. Something fundamentally broke between us, and that's when I realized I can't hold this marriage together any longer. We're in a sinking ship, and I'm the only one trying to patch the holes.

I'm so fucking tired.

As soon as I'm outside, my phone lights up with a text from Santiago. I quickly read the message and my heart lurches, but my decision has been a long time coming. I send a quick reply before stuffing my phone back into my purse. The hairs on the back of my neck stand on end, and

I'm no longer alone. Elias is next to me, handing something over to the valet driver, who nods and scurries away.

Elias's dark brown eyes bore into me. The devastation and confusion in his gaze nearly crumbles me. One look can't change months of unresolved issues and feelings of being unappreciated. I'm doing what needs to be done, even if it fucking hurts like a bullet to the heart.

I strengthen my resolve. The wind picks up, and I shiver as my hair blows behind my shoulders. From the corner of my eye, Elias shrugs off his jacket, but before he can hand it over, his car arrives, and I slip inside to avoid an awkward refusal. Freezing to death sounds like a better alternative to taking anything from him right now.

I fasten my seatbelt, forcing down the storm of pain, hurt, and confusion, burying it deep, and locking it away. I will not break. Not now.

The door opens, and Elias slips in without a sound. He buckles himself in, his gaze flickering toward me. I refuse to meet his heavy stare. Instead, I turn away, staring out the window as if the world outside might offer some kind of escape. The words I wish to say don't come to me.

A quiet sigh escapes him, barely audible over my pounding heart. Then, without a word, he shifts the car into drive and pulls away, the tension between us thicker than the silence.

Elias clears his throat more than once like he'll say something. Anything. But the silence only stretches out. I feel like I'm sitting next to a stranger not my husband. A man who should love me. When did he last tell me he loved me? I've always said it first. Have I seriously been so ignorant that I didn't notice all the cracks in our foundation until the house crashed down around us?

The entire fifteen-minute drive home is swallowed by thick and unyielding silence.

As Elias pulls up to our front gate, his frown sharpens, etched deep with confusion. The gate is wide open, an invitation to anyone, when it should be locked tight. My pulse races, an anxious beat echoing in my chest.

He doesn't know what this moment means.

But I do.

And I wish I didn't. I wish it never came to this, but here we are. We are reaching the final chapter of our book.

Our driveway isn't long—normally, it takes less than a minute to reach the house. But tonight, it stretches endlessly, each second dragging like an eternity. There's so much I want to say to him, but my anger from earlier has deserted me and leaves nothing but heartbreak in its place. If I speak, the tears will come, and I'll never be able to stop them.

When we finally reach the end of the driveway, my stomach twists.

We're not alone. Another car sits in the driveway.

"What the fuck?" Elias curses under his breath. He reaches over between my legs and my traitorous body, clearly unaware of the state of our relationship, heats for him. But that heat turns to stone-cold dread when something silver catches the light, shining as he pulls it out. My brain is slow to process what it is.

A gun.

Holy fucking shit. He thinks we're being robbed.

A small part of me loves that his first instinct is to make sure I'm safe.

And then I remember I'm pissed at him, and he's about to shoot my best friend. "What are you doing? Put that away! When did you get a gun?"

"I've always had a gun. You've just never seen it," he murmurs. His hand curls around the door handle as he pushes it open, but I grab his arm before he can get out.

"Stop! It's only Santiago and Noah doing what I asked them to do," I say. Elias tenses under my touch.

In slow motion, he turns his head to look at me. Those brown eyes I once fell in love with now burn with anger and pain, knocking the breath from my lungs. "And why are Santiago and Noah here, Catalina?"

My name on his lips is the catalyst.

The box I pushed my emotions into explodes, hitting me with the full force of anger, sadness, and regret—emotions I can't hide any longer. Sobs rack through my body, immobilizing me. Elias doesn't even try to reach for me; he's still rooted in his spot, one hand on the door and the other on the gun. Even though we are in the middle of a fight, I don't fear he'll hurt me. No matter how upset he is with me.

When I speak again, my voice is shaky and inaudible. "Because I need to leave you," I sob. "I love you so damn much, Elias, but I don't think you feel the same anymore. So, I have to love myself more."

"What the fuck does that mean? You think I don't love you? You think everything I do is because I don't love you?"

This is the most emotion he's expressed in months, but it comes too late. And it's not lost on me that he didn't say he loves me back. "I need space. Need to be out of your house—"

"Our house, Catalina. It's *our* house," he snaps.

"A house you bought because my *silly* little videos couldn't ever afford us something like this," I hiss, some of my earlier ire coming back. He winces at my words, much like I did when he diminished the value of my job. "You're working anyway, so it's not like you'll notice I'm gone." I can't keep the bitterness out of my words. "And I think you need to be without me for a while."

"I don't want to be without you, Catalina," he snarls.

"I want to believe that. I do. But your words and actions don't show it. I shouldn't have to threaten to leave you for you to give a damn about me."

Elias opens his mouth to snap back, but I don't want to hear it. My resolve is crumbling. I need to leave soon, or I'll talk myself into staying, and we will fall back into the same damn routine. I can't keep doing that to myself. I preach in my videos how women should be girl bosses who respect themselves and their bodies and always chase their happiness.

I've been ignoring my own advice for far too long.

Catching my attention, Santiago and Noah walk out of the house carrying two bags packed with my things. My time is officially up.

"I'm not spending Christmas alone. I hope your work is worth all of this." With those final words, I grip the door handle and push it open, stepping out into the cold night. Behind me, I feel Elias reach for me—hesitation, regret, and so many unsaid words hang between us. But just like every other time, in every other part of our lives, I slip through his fingers, leaving him behind.

"Catalina!" he calls.

I don't look back. I can't look back.

I keep my head high, telling myself I'm worth putting first.

The first snowflake falls, landing on the bridge of my nose. It feels like even the earth is crying for me.

The moment I reach Santiago, all the strength leaves my body. I fall into my best friend's arms, sobbing.

"Oh honey," he murmurs, his own voice hitching with emotion. He knows how hard this is.

"Let's get her into the car, babe," Noah says, and two sets of hands are on me, leading me to Santiago's car. Someone yells out my name, but it's lost as I'm guided into the back seat. The door shuts with a resounding thud. Santiago gets in on the other side, leaving Noah to drive. I'm grateful for my best friend and fall back into his arms.

Noah steers the car out of my driveway as the snow falls in thick, swirling flakes, slowly coating the world in white. I glance out the back window, my breath fogging the glass, and see Elias step out of the car. He stands there, motionless, watching us disappear into the storm.

For a fleeting moment, I see a man unraveling—a man just beginning to understand the weight of what he's losing.

Then the distance swallows him, and he's gone. Just like that.

I turn away from it all, pressing my face into Santiago's solid and warm chest. His arms wrap around me, anchoring me as the tears come—steady, unstoppable, and silent. The weight of heartbreak drags at every part of me, each breath heavier than the last. Slowly, exhaustion takes over, and I surrender to the darkness.

CHAPTER 4

CABIN IN THE SNOWY WOODS

Catalina

Gentle hands nudge me awake, pulling me from my dreamless slumber. Sleeping has been a mercy from reality where everything is crashing down around me. Santiago's kind face fills my foggy vision. A door opens from the front of the car, bringing in the blast of cold from outside, making me shiver.

"We're here," Santiago says gently, holding something out for me. My jacket. He must've grabbed it when I texted him I needed to get away from Elias. We drove through the night. Santiago and Noah had scheduled a romantic getaway in a cabin in Colorado, but they definitely didn't expect the extra baggage—mentally or physically.

"Noah just checked the lodge. The owners said they have an extra cabin available. Of course, you're welcome to stay with us—"

I shake my head before he can say another word. I can't keep leaning on him after everything I've already put him through. "I'll take the extra cabin," I whisper, my voice raw and hoarse from crying.

Reaching for the jacket, I slip it on and pull it tightly around myself, as if it might hold me together. Luckily, I think I've used up all of my tears. "Santi . . . I'm so sorry for all of this."

"Oh shush, honey. I'm not going to leave my best friend miserable on Christmas."

"You know you're always welcome to celebrate with us," Noah says from behind Santiago. He peeks around his husband, holding out a key for me, presumably to my cabin. At least I'll have my own space, so I'm not bringing down Santi and Noah. They're just being kind, and I will not drag them into the misery pit with me.

"Thank you. I'm just going to head in and rest a little longer."

Santiago nods understandingly. "Noah and I will check on you later. There's Wi-Fi, so maybe relax and stream a movie. We're all going out to dinner tonight, and I'm not taking no for an answer. We're going to be fucking jolly, even if I have to force you to do it."

Despite the heaviness weighing on me, a small smile breaks through. Hiding away and wallowing in my emotions would be easy—honestly, it's all I want to do— but maybe being around people who care about me and want to spend time with me, is what I need.

"Okay," I say softly. "Dinner sounds good."

Santiago's smile widens at my response. Noah steps forward and hands me my keys before motioning toward a cleared, narrow path, winding up a gentle hill. "Your cabin is on the left," he says warmly. "We're just next door, so if you need anything at all, don't hesitate to come find us."

I nod, even though I know I won't.

Unbuckling myself, I open the door and exit the car. Snowflakes kiss my eyelashes as my body shivers from the intense chill. It's so beautiful here. I've always loved a white Christmas, even though it looks different than I visioned. Elias has always been part of that dream, but thinking about my husband fills me with insurmountable grief. I push it down, grabbing my bags from Noah.

We walk in silence until we reach the top of the hill. I promise them I'll be ready for dinner, and then we part ways.

As I step through the door of the cabin, a wave of loneliness washes over me.

Inside, the warmth and beauty of the space momentarily ease the ache in my chest. The cabin is cozy and inviting, blanketed in the quiet hush of freshly fallen snow. I stand in a large, open room where soft golden light flickers from a stone fireplace. The fire crackles gently, heating the room. Surrounding the hearth are plush, over-sized couches draped in thick, knitted blankets and piled high with pillows. It's the perfect place to curl up and disappear for a while, which is exactly what I'm looking to do.

To the left, a charming kitchenette occupies one corner of the room. Wooden cabinets, a small stove, and a tiny round table set for two make it feel quaint and homey. On the right, a narrow hallway leads to a small bathroom and a bedroom. The door to the bedroom is slightly ajar, and I see the edge of a large bed covered in flannel sheets and more cozy blankets.

Despite the beauty and warmth around me, a quiet stillness settles. I'm alone and will be alone on Christmas.

I let my bags drop to the ground, exhaustion heavy on my chest. So many emotions and memories run through my mind.

I've never been one to keep a diary. I like the thought of it, but maintaining one seems like a burden. However, the want to document my life is the thing that got me into vlogging. A space I can freely express myself—at least on the vlogs I decide not to post. It's an outlet that has helped me in many aspects of my life. Something I turn to when things get tough, and I need to vent.

With slow strides, I sit on the couch, pulling my phone from my pocket. A dumb idea comes to me. The type of idea that's equivalent to drunk texting an ex. I'll probably regret it later, but it feels like the right decision in the moment. Plus, I have no one here to stop me. It's like the universe telling me to do the stupid thing.

I tap on my favorite social media app and scroll to Live. Propping my phone up on the table in front of me and after making sure I'm in frame, I click the button to begin streaming. The little indicator at the top shows over 500 people have joined, and the chat is popping off.

CATLOVER93: "HI."

XXTONYXX: "WHERE ARE YOU?"

GAMERGURL: "HIIIII."

I ignore them all.

"Hi beautiful people," I say, impressed my voice doesn't crack. However, my blood-shot eyes, unkempt hair, and puffy face are strong indicators that I've been crying. My followers aren't dumb. The chat fills with people asking me what's wrong, and I dig my nails into my thighs to center myself. I pretend I'm on a video call with my closest friends.

"I built my platform on authenticity, showing you the realness of my life. And the reality is, I haven't been completely honest with you. Despite the happiness and joy I try to convey in my videos, I've been feeling lost and alone for a long time now . . . maybe more than I'm willing to admit."

As expected, the chat fills with people speculating about what's going on. Everything from losing a parent or friend to being unhappy in a plus-size body. I roll my eyes at the latter one because the fatphobic people will always find a way to bring my body into the conversation.

"Christmas is my favorite time of year, but this year is hard. Love is hard." I release a breathy laugh, shaking my head. "Actually, Christmas can be really . . . weird. It's beautiful and full of magic for some people and heavy as hell for others. I don't think I ever realized it until this year. The magic feels . . . lost.

"People don't talk enough about how you can love someone and still feel lonely next to them. Or how things can stop working. Love doesn't always leave in a big dramatic way. Sometimes it just . . . fades. Quietly. And that's fucking hard. Especially, if you're still full of love for that person, but it's killing you inside."

I make the mistake of looking down at the comments, reading a few.

> BOOKISHLOVER: "OH MY GOD, DID SHE LEAVE HER HUSBAND?"

> GYMDUDE1: "THE MAN THAT MARRIED HER GOT HIS BAG AND LEFT. DON'T BLAME HIM."

> NESSA.23: "ARE WE SUPPOSED TO BE SAD THAT A RICH WOMAN IS CRYING ON SOCIAL MEDIA?"

I shouldn't have looked down. The cruel comments do little to ease the pain, but I can't stop reading them. It's like a train wreck happening in slow motion. I should stop talking live on the internet, but I'm desperate for someone —*anyone*—to hear me.

"I'm not gonna get into all the details. I know it's annoying when influencers, especially ones that have put their relationship online, say that, so I am sorry. But I will say having someone fall out of love with you? That shit *hurts*. It's even worse when it happens around the holidays when everyone else is posting matching pajamas and kissing under the mistletoe."

A tear slips out before I can stop it. Apparently, I do have a few more tears to spare.

"This isn't me looking for pity. I just . . . I guess I wanted someone to sit with me today. And maybe remind someone else out there that it's okay if your Christmas doesn't look like a Hallmark movie. You're not broken. You're not unlovable. You're not alone. I'm sitting right there with you. Thank you for listening."

This time I ignore the comments as I end the video, cutting the screen to black. A message pops up, asking if I want to share the video on my page. Knowing I've done enough damage for one night, I click "no."

I silence my phone before deciding just to turn it off completely. I'm certain there are discussions about what I meant in my video, but I don't care what people come up with. I feel purged and vindicated for saying my piece. Maybe my words resonated with someone else spending Christmas alone.

If my words help a single soul, I don't regret it. Not even a little.

CHAPTER 5

LONELY IN DECEMBER

Elias

Having someone fall out of love with you? That shit hurts.

Catalina's words replay in my head, driving the dagger further into my heart. The quiver in her lip and the way she choked out the words like they physically pained her fucking broke me. This woman—*my* woman is hurting because of me. She's crying because of me.

When the notification saying Catalina was live popped up, I fumbled to open it. I'm not like my wife; social media might as well be written in code. It took me way too long to figure out how to even join the Live, and when I finally did, I couldn't hear a damn thing. My phone volume was all the way down. Of course it was. By the time I turned it up, the first thing that hit me wasn't her words but rather the raw pain in her voice. I wasn't ready for that pain. Not even close.

How had I been so fucking ignorant and missed so much?

When she cut the video, it felt like losing her all over again. My finger hovers over her picture, desperate to touch her and have her back in front of me.

As I scroll through her feed, I watch my wife come to life photo after photo, video after video. On the surface, she looks radiant. To everyone else, Catalina is glowing. She's full of laughter, light, and confidence. A goddess. Untouchable.

But I know better.

I've been by her side since we were kids. We got married fresh out of high school, clinging to each other and a handful of dreams. We didn't have a dime to our names back then, but we had love. We believed it could carry us into a better future. I promised her I'd build a future where she'd never have to struggle again as long as I was around.

I know her better than anyone. And now, I see things everyone else overlooks. They cut deeper than I ever thought they would. I notice every look, every silence, every shift in her breathing.

Her smile doesn't quite reach her eyes anymore. There's a dull, hollow kind of sadness she tries to hide behind perfect angles and filtered light. But it's haunting the hell out of me.

I'm the one who put it there.

My phone buzzes, lighting up with a call. For a moment, my heart lurches because I think it's my wife. The fantasy shatters when I see it's César and disappointment washes over me.

I have half a mind to ignore the call, but he could be

calling about work. Old habits die hard. With a curse, I answer and bring the phone up to my ear. "What?"

Laughter echoes on the other end, irritating me more. "Who pissed in your cereal, cabrón?"

"Is there something you need?" I grit out.

"Actually, I called to check on you. I'm glad I did." César pauses. "I saw the video, man."

Shame and embarrassment war within me. It's one thing to have lost my wife and quite another having people know I fucked up. I shouldn't be surprised César saw the video. The man knows and sees everything—a rather annoying quality. He knows shit no one wants him to know. Considering Catalina spoke for the whole world to hear, I can hardly blame him this time.

I don't blame her either.

I'm a private person and didn't know how I'd feel to have our lives out in the open for all to see. I've worked too many damn PR nightmares to know this could end badly, but Catalina was adamant that this is what she wanted to do. So, I supported her, but it didn't make it any fucking easier.

Now I'm sitting alone in this damn house Catalina decorated to look like Christmas exploded all over it. Everything reminds me of her. Hell, everything smells like her, too. It's agony to feel her around me, but not physically have her. My punishment.

César doesn't speak, but I hear him breathing. The bastard is waiting for me to speak, but each word feels like a heavy burden I'm not sure I can lift on my own. I sigh, leaning back against the counter and scanning the large, empty house.

"She's gone, man. She's really gone." Saying the words makes it real. How can I fix everyone else's messes for a living, but I can't do shit when it comes to my own life? Fate's a fickle bitch.

"Yeah, she is," he agrees. César doesn't bullshit me. He's not afraid to speak his mind, even if it'll piss me off. We clash like brothers—loud, stubborn, and unafraid to hit where it hurts. But beneath the arguments and sharp words, there's a bond just as fierce. We look out for each other and protect one another like only brothers can.

I don't expect him to say more, so when he does, my body tenses.

"Listen, I'm not gonna coddle you, Eli. You didn't just lose her overnight. This didn't come outta nowhere."

I bristle as heat rises in my chest. What the fuck does he know? He might know me better than most—hell, maybe as well as Catalina—but he doesn't know my marriage. He doesn't see the sacrifices I make every damn day to provide for my wife. "I was working to build something for us. I thought that mattered to her." My voice comes out sharper than I mean it to.

César isn't affected by my tone. He's worked with as many stubborn clients as I have, so he's used to people talking to him defensively. "It did, but being present matters more. Love doesn't live on paychecks, cabrón. You were building a future while she was drowning in the present *alone*. How many times have I told you to go home? To stop working so many hours? You're a damn good lawyer, but you've been a shitty husband."

My body tenses, preparing for a fight. The urge to punch something and expel the pent-up rage brewing inside me is strong. It pisses me off more because . . . he's right. The fucker said he would not coddle me, and he's telling me shit I don't want to hear. No matter how much I wish it wasn't, it was the truth.

"I didn't see it. I thought she was okay," I reply after the anger and desire to throttle him simmers.

"You didn't want to see it. There's a difference. She gave you signs, Eli. How many dates have you blown off? What about those trips she was taking for her social media? You don't think she would have preferred you to go with her? You just ignored 'em. Kept pushing everything off, thinking you had time. Newsflash! You didn't, and now it's caught up to you."

"Fuck, kick me in the balls why don't you? When the hell did you become a relationship expert? I don't remember you locking down a wife."

"Don't worry about me. I'm keeping my options open. Now, don't change the subject, fucker. What are you going to do?" he asks.

"I can't let her leave," I say automatically. Catalina is mine. She's mine to love, and I'd be damned if I ever let another man take her from me.

"No shit. So instead of moping around your house, why don't you do something? She's running, so you gotta chase her. Don't just show up with flowers and a sad face, expecting her to fall into your arms. *Fight*. Rebuild what you broke, piece by piece. Listen, show up, and *change*. I'm telling you this as a friend and business partner, you need to put her first, not your damn job. It's a bad look for a prominent attorney to be tangled in a mess he can't fix."

Damn this man. I know he's right. César is too fucking smart. He's always been a romantic. A man who loves love and the women he's with. Despite his knowledge in this area, I don't see him securing a wife yet.

I know it's my bitterness speaking. One thing still troubles me, burning in the back of my mind. "What if it's too late?"

I imagine César shrugging. "Then at least you go down swinging. At least she knows you *finally* saw her and you didn't just let her slip away without a damn fight. Haven't you learned that in our line of work? You fight no matter how many things are stacked against you. You fight, and you fight like hell.

"But," he adds, "leave that fucking ego and temper at the house. No woman wants that. You go in humble, shut up, and listen. Don't be an idiot, brother. Get your woman back." Without another word, the line goes dead.

I sit alone in the quiet, staring at the dim glow of the Christmas tree. Catalina put this one up the day after Halloween because Christmas has always been her favorite holiday.

For the first time since she left last night, the silence doesn't feel suffocating. It still hurts—God, it hurts—but beneath the ache, something else flickers to life.

César is right. I can't undo the past, but I can fight for the future. For her.

Of course, finding her would be a breach of trust since I have her phone tracked. In my line of work, I've seen and heard some crazy shit, and I needed to ensure I knew where Catalina always was. I've been tracking her phone for almost five years. I suspect she knows I do but has never called me out on it. She can track me, too, but I don't think she realizes she has that app on her phone.

I don't have all the answers yet, but I have a direction and a purpose. No more excuses, no more hiding behind work or good intentions. If Catalina ever gives me another chance, she's getting a man who shows up with both feet in and heart first. If that's the man she needs, then fuck it, that's the man I'll become.

I'm coming for you, Catalina. And I'm not letting you slip away from me again.

CHAPTER 6

SANTA'S ROSES

Catalina

I hadn't meant to miss dinner last night, but sometime after my impromptu live, I fell asleep and woke up the following morning to five missed calls and seven texts from Santi.

Are you doing okay?

Catalina, we saw the live, are you okay?

Please say you're okay.

You're not answering. Noah's going over to check.

He checked! You're asleep. You must be really tired because you didn't budge when he came in. We're coming by in the morning, though.

None of the missed texts or calls came from Elias.

I guess I expected too much. By leaving I had hoped Elias would finally understand just how serious I am. I thought maybe he would have called to apologize and talk about our future together. But he's been silent since I got into Santiago's car and drove away from him. I don't know about him, but that was the fucking hardest thing I've ever had to do.

I hate questioning if I did the right thing or not.

Knowing Santi and Noah will storm into my cabin at any moment, I head to the bathroom to change and look presentable.

Ten minutes later, the front door opens, and Santiago calls out for me. "Catalina! You better not be hiding from me."

"Now, why would I be hiding from you, Santi?" I ask, stepping out of the bathroom.

Santiago lets out a shriek and leaps into the air, like a cat that's just caught sight of its shadow. Noah bursts into laughter at his husband's dramatic reaction, receiving a playful smack to the chest.

"Why are you sneaking up on me?" Santi demands, panting as he presses a hand to his chest and glares between Noah and I as if we had plotted to scare him behind his back.

"I can't really sneak up on you when you're the one breaking into my cabin," I point out.

"Fair point," Santiago agrees. "We were just worried about you. After the live last night. . . I don't know, Cat. All that pain in your voice broke my heart."

My cheeks heat as a flood of embarrassment washes over me. "Yeah . . . maybe that wasn't my smartest move, but I don't regret it. It's how I felt. And since Elias isn't listening, I need someone to hear me."

"We hear you, love," Noah says, moving to stand next to his husband. "You're not alone."

I smile and choke back emotions that threaten to consume me. "I appreciate and love both of you," I say. "Sometimes it's hard to be around two people so much in love when your marriage is going up in flames."

Santiago gives me a sympathetic expression before hugging me. I happily accept, falling into my best friend's arms. "I love you, and I'm so thankful for our friendship, even if I have to pay you to hang out with me."

"Shut up," he laughs, squeezing me harder. "I could be charging you a lot more to hang out with you, so consider yourself lucky."

"Are you both ready to go to the lodge and get breakfast?" Noah asks, interrupting our hug fest as my stomach growls. I don't remember eating at all yesterday, too consumed by grief. Now my body is angry at me. I also desperately need coffee. Like now.

"Let me just get my shoes on, and we can go," I call, heading to my suitcase when someone knocks on the door. I freeze, looking back at the guys to see if they are expecting anyone, but they wear the same looks of confusion.

"Uhm, are we expecting someone?" Santiago asks. "Or did we walk into a horror movie and are about to be killed?"

"Santi!" I hiss. I hadn't been thinking about *that*, but now that's all I can think about.

"Well, someone needs to open the door, and it's not going to be me!" Santiago says, moving behind the couch.

He crouches down, peering over the top. "I'll stay here. I vote Noah goes."

"Me? Why the fuck do I have to get killed first?" he hisses.

"I guess I'll be the brave one," I mutter, rolling my eyes. "But if I die, you better make content about it."

Santiago salutes me. "I'll go live at your funeral."

With that sobering thought weighing on me, I slowly inch toward the door as another knock echoes from the other side. A quiet, tentative voice in the back of my mind wonders if it's Elias. Did he come all this way to see me? To apologize?

The possibility makes my heart flutter and ache all at once. But even if it is him . . . do I really want to face him right now? Maybe it's still too soon. Maybe I'm not ready. Maybe I still need more time to breathe on my own.

Maybe . . .

All thoughts of Elias die when I crack open the door and see red. Literally red. A large Santa look alike stands there, complete with a large belly and full beard. He's holding a bouquet of at least three dozen flowers.

When he laughs, his whole body shakes. "Ho, ho, ho! You must be Catalina."

I hear movement from behind me before Santiago comes into view and yanks the door all the way open. "Holy shit, it's Santa!"

"Watch your mouth around Santa, young man. You wouldn't want to end up on my naughty list," Santa says, winking at Santi. My friend just makes a face, while Noah hides a snicker behind us.

I'm certain Santiago flips Santa off.

"Um, yeah, I'm Catalina," I say, trying to peer past him, half-expecting to spot the cabin owners nearby.

Maybe this is just some festive tradition they do every Christmas. Snow has fallen again, and soft flakes drift down to blanket the already white landscape with another shimmering layer. With Santa standing right in front of me and the world transformed into a winter wonderland, it feels like we've stepped straight into the North Pole.

"Someone says you have been a really good girl this year and wanted to make sure I personally delivered these roses to you. Said they are your favorite." Santa beams, handing over the bouquet.

My body freezes. Red roses. My favorite kind. And only one person has ever sent me *these* flowers.

Grabbing the bouquet is no easy task considering how damn big it is, but I manage to get my hands around the bottom with only a few pricks from the thorns.

"Is there a note?" Santiago asks, leaning in to look. He pulls back after a moment and shakes his head. "No note."

"Who are these from?" I ask Santa.

The jolly man simply laughs, his belly shaking. "You'll see," he says with a wink that only deepens my confusion. Then, with a flourish, he reaches into his pocket and pulls out an elegant card trimmed in gold. "You've also been gifted a special breakfast for you and your friends," he explains, handing it to me. "Present this to the woman at the lodge's front desk. She'll take care of the rest and escort you to your destination."

Like a fool, I just stare at the card in disbelief. Santi clears his throat before reaching for it. "Thanks Santa. We'll be using this now."

"Good, good!" he says far too cheerfully for this early in the morning. "Merry Christmas, Mrs. Ayala." Santa laughs again before descending the steps. He walks back to his sleigh—AKA Jeep—and speeds back down the trail going faster than what seems safe.

"Think Santa had one too many eggnogs?" Santi mumbles.

My gaze flickers back down to the roses. They smell beautiful, like summer. Back when Elias and I first got married, we scraped together just enough money to rent our first apartment. The only furniture we had were folding tables we stole from our parents' garages and an old TV Elias found in the trash and restored. Despite having very little money to our name and a barely furnished apartment, every Friday night Elias brought home a dozen roses.

"Cariño, one day you'll have a garden to grow your own roses. Until then, I'll bring them home to you," he would say. Even though I knew every Friday he'd bring home roses, I always teared up. It was such a sweet, thoughtful gift. And now, I can't remember the last time he bought me flowers for something other than my birthday. I don't realize how much I miss it until they are in my hands again.

These had to be from Elias. Who else would send me a random bouquet of roses in the middle of nowhere? But that only raises another question—how did he even know where I am? I've always suspected he was tracking my phone, and this pretty much confirms it.

Maybe I *should* be angry that my husband is basically stalking me . . . but instead, I feel a strange sense of comfort. I'm so starved for his affection that the idea of him caring enough to find me—no matter how questionable the method—makes my heart ache in the best kind of way.

Both men are looking at me when I tear my gaze away

from the roses. They both wear the same expression of not knowing if they should be happy or mad for me.

"It's from Elias," I say quickly. "I mean, I think it is anyway. Unless one of you sent it?"

Santi and Noah shake their heads as I suspected.

"What do I do?" It's a dumb question. This is a decision I should make on my own, but my heart and mind are at war with one another. My heart wants to run back to Elias and never leave him again, while my head tells me roses aren't going to fix months of neglect.

"Well," Santi says and holds up the invitation, "we are going to have a bomb ass breakfast, and you're going to take pictures and videos of it for B-roll footage. If Elias has any more surprises awaiting you, we will deal with it then. But right now, I'm starving. And nothing tastes better than breakfast paid for by someone else."

"And what Santi fails to mention is if you want to talk about Elias and where your head's at during breakfast, we can," Noah adds.

I don't know what I did to deserve these two, but I'm thankful they're in my life. This would all be so much harder if I didn't have Santi and Noah to lean on.

They are right. We shouldn't waste a perfectly good breakfast. If Elias knows where I'm at, then he can continue to reach out. I've done enough.

Placing the bouquet down on the kitchen table, I quickly slip into my boots. "No boy talk. Just breakfast. Then the two of you are going to leave me alone, so you can have the romantic getaway you planned."

"You're the boss," Santi says with a grin. When he turns to look at Noah, his face softens with so much love it makes my chest tighten. A tenderness exists between them that's impossible to miss, and I feel a quiet pang of jealousy stir in me. Noah leans in and presses a gentle kiss to Santi's lips. It's a soft, public-appropriate gesture, but it's intimate enough that I instinctively look away, not wanting to intrude on the moment.

"Okay!" Santi said once they break away. "Let's go see what apology breakfast Elias has in store for you." And with that, we head out of my cabin.

CHAPTER 7

GHOSTS OF CHRISTMAS PAST

Elias

I sit quietly in the far corner of the lodge's only fine dining restaurant, nursing a lukewarm cup of coffee. It's the price I pay to keep my seat without drawing attention. Every time the hostess walks through the foyer, my heart skips a beat, hoping she's escorting Catalina. By now, she must have received the over-the-top Santa—a festive gesture she usually adores—I had delivered to her cabin. She should've also seen the invitation for breakfast.

She probably suspects I'm here. The roses had been a dead giveaway. They are a symbol of our past and that I remember how things used to be before work took over my life and she took the back burner.

Finding Catalina hadn't been difficult. I tracked her location shortly after getting off the phone with César with no plan in place other than to get my wife back. I had a ten-hour drive through the start of a gnarly snow storm to think about what I wanted to do. Bottom line, I wanted to give Catalina the ability to control the moment. I'm still allowing her space.

For now.

Finding her cabin had proven slightly more difficult than expected. But a well-placed smile and a few charming words to the elderly woman managing the lodge did the trick. She was more than happy to point me in the right direction. Catalina had her own cabin—perfect. Sharing space with Santi and Noah would've complicated things, considering what I planned to do with her to show her just how sorry I am.

Another fifteen minutes go by and I start to worry. There's a chance she won't want anything to do with me or the gifts I've arranged. César said I need to accept that losing her, even after all of this, is a possibility. Except, it's not. Catalina is mine. She has been mine since I saw her during Freshman Boot Camp, smiling and laughing with all her friends. Everything about her drew me in. That beautiful woman didn't seem attainable, but she fell in love with me.

I swore I would never lose her love. And yet, I'm close to doing just that.

A feminine laugh steals my attention, and I glance up to see the hostess walking in. My breath catches when I see Catalina. It hasn't been long since she's left, but it may as well have been months. She's wearing tight black leggings that show off her perfect ass. My girl has never been shy in showing off her curves, and she shouldn't be. I fucking love her body, and I love how much she loves her body, despite not fitting into the conventional beauty standards.

Fuck them. My girl *is* the beauty standard.

Catalina isn't alone, of course. Santi and Noah trail behind her, laughing at something the hostess must've said. She leads them to a table on the opposite side of the restaurant, right by a massive window that frames the snow-covered mountains like a painting. From where I'm sitting, I have a clear, unobstructed view of my wife, but thanks to the placement of nearby tables and the carefully arranged decor, she can't see me. This is as I planned it. I'm not ready to reveal myself, and Catalina still needs time.

The hostess doesn't leave menus because I've already paid for a buffet breakfast. A waiter comes by and gives the three of them mimosas and pull-apart cinnamon bread to snack on before their food comes out. The one downside to being so far away from Catalina is that I can't hear their conversation.

My wife is smiling, but it's not her usual smile. Sadness lingers in her eyes. Sadness that I placed. If all things go according to plan this weekend, that sadness will never enter her eyes again. I refuse to accept any other outcome. I didn't get where I am today by being a passive man, content for life to pass him by.

The same waiter that is taking care of Catalina's table comes up to me with a fresh pot of coffee. "Can I top you off, sir?" he asks, briefly glancing at what I'm staring at. I have the primal urge to gauge his eyes out, but that behavior is frowned upon. Lucky bastard.

I put down my coffee, nodding once. The waiter tops me off with more lukewarm coffee that is far too watered-down for the price they're charging me for it.

"Do you still want me to give Mrs. Ayala the envelope?" he asks.

The second part of my plan.

"Only once breakfast is done. Make no mention of who sent it to her." I've gone over this several times before, hoping it sticks. I'm not ready for her to know I'm here, even if she suspects it.

"Yes, sir. Can I get you anything else?"

Again, I shake my head, dismissing him, and I watch as he goes back over to Catalina's table. My girl is on her phone, taking photos of the food and view. She then passes the phone to Santi to take a picture of her.

She's breathtaking.

I need to tell her that more often.

I watch like the obsessed fucker I am as they talk in hushed whispers. Sometimes they are laughing so loud that a few people glance over at them. They can judge all they want, but it doesn't seem to bother anyone at my wife's table.

Their breakfast arrives in a flurry of clinking plates drifting with steam and mountains of food—scrambled and golden eggs, crispy, glistening strips of bacon, and brown to perfection hash browns. Fluffy biscuits drenched in thick, peppered gravy sit beside a towering stack of waffles dusted with powdered sugar and crowned with a pat of melting butter. My mouth waters, but I'm too worked up to eat right now. Coffee is my limit.

Catalina picks up her phone again, angling it to capture the spread. After a few quick shots, she smiles in satisfaction. But then, something shifts. With her fingers still on the screen, her smile falters.

She lifts her head.

Her gaze scans the room slowly, searching—purposeful and alert as if she's expecting someone. As if she's looking for me.

For one breathless moment, her eyes drift toward my side of the restaurant. My pulse quickens. Does she feel me watching her? Does she sense me here, hidden just beyond her line of sight?

I'm here, cariño.

She looks away because she can't see me. She turns her attention back to her plate, reaching for her fork. Just like that, I'm invisible again. A mere ghost.

Exactly how it has to be. For now. Even if I'm dying to have her in my arms.

Breakfast is a mostly quiet affair, at least for Catalina. Noah and Santi do most of the talking, their voices weaving easily together in laughter. They make an effort to include her, tossing questions her way or looping her into jokes, but the dynamic is unmistakable. There's always something off about a trio, especially when two of them are in love. No matter how kind they are, the third person inevitably feels like an extra piece, orbiting a world they don't quite belong to.

Catalina doesn't say it, but the truth sits heavy between bites: she wasn't part of the original plan. Her presence feels like an afterthought—a convenient way to get her out of town and out of reach from me. This trip isn't about her.

It's their romantic getaway. She's just tagging along.

Their breakfast lasts for nearly an hour, each of them eventually leaning back with contented smiles and hopefully full stomachs. It's the perfect moment to proceed with the next step. I know Catalina well enough to recognize how important this next gift will be. If she accepts it, the rest of my plan will fall into place. And I believe she will.

The entire table has been booked for a luxurious spa

day complete with four uninterrupted hours of indulgence, pampering, and relaxation. While they're being tended to, I'll prepare the last, and most important, part of my plan.

The server catches my eye, and I nod, before he heads over to the table with the invitation in hand. Catalina's eyes widen as the server hands over the card that has their reservations and vouchers for the spa. Her eyes shoot up and she scans the room again, searching harder this time.

There's no doubt in my mind she knows I'm here.

Watching. Waiting.

The three of them engage in an intense conversation, probably weighing whether or not they should accept the spa package. It doesn't take long for them to come to an agreement because soon Catalina is passing out the vouchers, and the three of them are leaving. I watch a little longer and breathe a sigh of relief when I see Catalina disappear down the hallway toward the spa.

"She seemed excited about the spa, sir," the server says, having approached while I was preoccupied watching my wife. "Is there anything else?"

"Nothing." I dig through my pocket and toss down a hundred—far more than what I owe for the coffee.

"I'll be right back with your change, sir."

"Keep it."

"Wow, really?" The man grins like I've bestowed the best gift upon him. "Thank you."

If he says anything else, I don't catch it. Maybe he thinks I'm an asshole—honestly, he wouldn't be wrong—but I don't have time to care about that right now. I've got a lot to get done before Catalina gets back to the cabin, and I won't waste a second.

Tonight, I'm going to prove my wife comes first. I've

been shit at keeping that in mind, but after this, my wife will never again doubt my love for her.

She'll know, without question, that I love her more than anything else in this damn world.

CHAPTER 8

IS THAT A YETI?

Catalina

Hiking back to the cabin after four hours of getting pampered and rubbed down with every oil and crème the lodge possesses makes me feel like I'm a seal slipping across ice. Each precarious step is one wrong move away from falling flat on my face, and that would suck because the facial from earlier is making my skin glow like a disco ball.

"So, do you want to talk about the elephant in the room? Or the elf on the shelf if we're being festive?" Santiago asks, also struggling to trek up the path to our cabins.

I shake my head, not quite ready to voice my thoughts. Honestly, I'm unsure if I could. Elias can't be away from work; he can't possibly have time to come out here. But he's spoiling me to make up for his absence. The question is why?

If he's trying to win me back, gifts are nice, but they aren't an apology or an acknowledgment of my feelings. Gifts are a bandage on an open, bloody wound. I appreciate his effort, but this isn't going to magically fix everything for us.

"Okay," Santi says slowly. "Do you want to hang out in our cabin and maybe watch a movie?"

"You're sweet, Santi, but I'm not butting in on anymore of your trip." Before he can argue with me, I bump his shoulder, nearly toppling us over onto Noah. "Don't tell me I'm not third wheeling because I so am. I want to just go back to the cabin and sort through my thoughts and emotions."

"Perhaps not on a Live this time?" Santi grins sheepishly.

"I don't regret that," I say. "But no Lives this time. Just me."

Shortly after and by some miracle, we reach the end of our trail, stopping at the fork separating our cabins.

"Are you sure you'll be okay?" Santi asks.

His heart is too pure, and I love him for checking in on me, but I want him to enjoy his Christmas vacation with his husband alone. "I'll be fine. And if I'm not, I know where to find you."

Santi assesses me, biting his lip once before nodding and pulling me in for a hug. "Love you. I'll edit the content from the spa sometime today and schedule it to drop tomorrow at noon."

"And then no work," I reprimand, not wanting him to do this in the first place, but Santi insisted.

"You're the boss." He squeezes me one last time and pulls back. "Now hurry and go inside. It's too damn cold out here, and the snow is piling up."

He's not wrong. At least a foot of fluffy white snow, if not more, blankets the ground. It looks like a scene from a Thomas Kincaid portrait; all it's missing is a cute frozen lake.

Santiago and Noah wave one final time before heading back to their cabin hand-in-hand.

Not wanting to be lost in the snow alone, I hurry toward the porch, my boots crunching against the frozen ground. As I reach the top step, I slow down, noticing something that makes my stomach twist. My hand stretches toward the front door and pauses mid-air. The door is open just enough for the bitter wind to catch the edge and creak it back and forth like an ominous warning.

I blink, startled. That's not right.

A chill creeps up my spine, and it has nothing to do with the cold. I stare at the door, my fingers now trembling as they hover near the frame. Did I forget to close it? No—I *know* I closed it. I remember pulling it shut, turning the knob, and hearing the familiar click before we left. I *had* to have. Right?

But now . . . doubt worms its way in. Maybe I didn't shut it all the way. Maybe I was distracted. Or maybe—no, that's ridiculous. Still, I can't shake the unease pressing down on me like the snow-heavy sky above.

I'm either walking into a snow cabin killer or another surprise from Elias.

Either way, I'm not ready.

Feeling like every dumbass character in a scary movie, I push open the door and brace myself.

I stop dead in my tracks.

In the middle of my cabin is an eight-foot-tall Christmas tree, decorated in ornaments—nothing with monetary value, only sentimental value. I've collected these ornaments over the years on different trips, from family members who made them for me, or from when Elias and I made together before we had the money to buy our own.

The lights are a warm, white light against the forest green of the tree's needles. The angel passed down from my mother rests on top. She's seen better days, face nearly wiped clean and dress stained from years of adorning our tree. She's just as beautiful as I remember from my childhood.

The tree isn't the only new decoration in the cabin. Tinsel and gold streamers dangle from the ceiling beams, catching the light and creating a shimmering effect like a sky full of stars. Wrapped presents are scattered throughout the room adding bursts of color, and large red ribbons are tied neatly to the window frames, giving the space a festive, cheerful warmth.

A fresh batch of chocolate chip cookies sit on the table next to another gold letter. I take a tentative step forward, half expecting Elias to jump out of the shadows and surprise me. But he doesn't. Because he isn't here. He's at work, and I'm alone in the cabin.

When I reach the table, I pick up the letter, turning it over to see Elias's handwriting on the back. It's not a long message. Just one short message.

I want to fix this. Leave your front door open at 8 p.m. Close it only if I've ruined us beyond repair.

I reread the words until I can make sense of them. Why would he want me to keep the door open? Does this mean . . . No, surely he's not here. Never in our marriage has Elias taken a spontaneous trip and time off work.

My eyes snap up to the nearest clock.

7:55 p.m.

Just five minutes.

Five minutes to determine my future. It doesn't seem like a long time as a second passes with each tick of the clock, and I'm that much closer to my future. What does my future look like?

I want to continue to inspire and uplift plus-size women.

I want to travel and experience different cultures.

I want a family, not necessarily children but a few pets and someone that loves me.

I want Elias . . . but does my husband *deserve* me?

Two minutes have passed.

I don't know if he does. I don't know if we can fix everything that has been broken. There's so much history between us. A love so fierce I never thought it would burn out. I still feel it deep inside me, begging to be let free again.

Another minute.

I stare at the door, knowing I could close it and walk away. Choose a new path, a new purpose where I no longer have to fight or ache. But the truth is, I don't want a life without Elias. I love him too much. I'm not willing to throw years of love and memories down the drain without fighting one last time.

Still, I can't keep going down the path we're on. If we continue like this—misunderstanding, hurting, drifting—he *will* lose me. Not in some sudden, dramatic way, but in slow, irreversible pieces. And that might be even worse.

But . . . maybe there's still a chance. Maybe he's finally listening. Maybe now, with everything out in the open, we can finally fix what's broken.

My time is up.

I hurry to the window by the door and look out. A

large, dark figure walks swiftly in the shadows, heading straight to my cabin.

This better not be a damn yeti.

The figure approaches, and the light from the porch illuminates the side of his face. My breath lurches, heart pounding in my chest.

Elias is here. Just beyond the door. I can hardly believe it.

I keep waiting to wake up, to find out this is just a dream conjured by longing and exhaustion. But it's real.

He left work. He came for me. Dressed in black like some dark, brooding knight. my husband is standing only a few feet away. He looks heartbreakingly handsome, and the sight of him makes my chest ache.

Even through the haze of my raw anger and hurt, my heart reaches for him. I wish I could shut it off and silence the part of me that still loves him so deeply, but I can't. Love doesn't come with a switch. And right now, my love is tangled with pain, pulsing just beneath the surface.

He takes the stairs two at a time and stops at the top of the porch. I hold my breath.

I see him. His beautiful face twisted, no longer calm or collected. It's a storm of emotion—pain, confusion, and something dangerously close to despair. Hurt and anger flash in his eyes like lightning.

He stands there, frozen in place as if he's afraid that taking a single step forward might shatter everything between us.

Why isn't he moving? Why isn't he saying anything?

Then I notice it.

The door is closed. The wind must have pulled it shut behind me without me realizing.

Fuck!

I scramble back, running to the door. I'm hit with a jolt of cold air as the door swings open.

I stop inches away from Elias. He stares at me like he's already lost me.

"The door was closed," I whisper. It's the only thing my brain can think to say to my husband of ten years. He feels more like a stranger than my husband, and that hurts most of all.

Elias doesn't speak. He takes a step forward, and I take a step back. He doesn't stop until he's inside the cabin, his intimidating figure darkening the entrance. He shuts the door and sweeps his gaze around before falling on me again.

"Tell me you want me to go," he says. Elias moves closer, and I back into a wall. His large frame cages me in, and my body shivers in anticipation and something else . . . like need.

"Tell me to go, Catalina," he repeats. His warm breath hits my cheek. He's so close, I can smell his peppermint aftershave and feel his warmth. It takes everything in my power to stand tall.

I need to say something—*anything*—but the words catch in my throat. For a moment, I'm completely frozen. Elias is standing right in front of me, so real and close it makes my pulse stutter. After all the silence and space between us, he's here. Today, he showered me with gifts—thoughtful, unexpected reminders that he still knows me. He still cares, and now, he's shown up in person when I needed someone most.

I'm still angry. Hurt. Confused.

A few gifts won't fix our marriage. But his presence is so solid and familiar. Something inside me starts to soften, not enough to forgive yet, but enough to listen.

"Catalina—"

"I didn't close the door," I blurt out, watching him tense. It's his turn to freeze, waiting for me to continue. "I was going to open it. I . . . I think the wind might have closed it."

For a moment we look at each other in silence. Something fizzles between us that neither of us can control.

He moves first. Or maybe I do. Our lips come together in a heated, needy kiss that has me gripping his arms to keep myself up. His tongue sweeps across my bottom lip, making me moan. I part for him, and he claims my mouth. He kisses me without restraint, like there's nothing between us. My body fills with pent up desire which I haven't experienced in so long.

Because he has been neglecting me and our marriage.

The thought is a douse of cold water, breaking me free from my horny fog. I move my hands to his chest, hearing his deep intake of breath. I muster all my strength.

Then I push him away.

CHAPTER 9

IT'S ALWAYS BEEN YOU

Elias

I stagger back. Not from the force of the push, but out of confusion.

Catalina's eyes are wide, full of pain. When the first tear falls, a dagger enters my heart. César said this would be hard. I knew this would be hard, but I didn't expect the weight of her tears to feel this heavy. I know I'm the reason for them.

"What are you doing here, Elias?" she asks, her voice tight. She crosses the room, putting distance between us. It's as if an invisible barrier forms, keeping me out of reach. "You think showing up and handing me gifts is going to fix everything?"

I know it won't, but a small, naïve part of me had hoped it would ease some of the pain I've created. "The gifts were to get you out of the cabin so I could—" I gesture around at my shoddy attempt at decorating.

Catalina has always been better at creating beautiful displays in our home. I had little time and very few things to work with, so I did what I could.

Catalina crosses her arms over her chest, which is fucking distracting because it pushes her tits up obscenely. Perhaps this is my torture. Every second spent not touching her is punishment. If I reach out now, I'm certain she'll push me off again. I'm one to enjoy rough sex but not when Catalina is truly pissed at me.

"I'm here to listen and to fix what I can. I fucked up."

"Yeah, you did," she snaps, the ire in her voice makes me frown.

I clamp down my anger. That won't serve me here.

"I didn't come to argue," I say quietly, tucking my hands into my pockets. "I just . . . needed to say I'm sorry for everything. I should've been there for you."

I let the first of what I'm sure will be many apologies hang between us. Catalina looks away as if trying to compose herself and find the right words.

"You think it's just about you being gone?" she says after a tense silence. Her voice is calm, but tight with something deeper—hurt or resentment, maybe both. "You weren't just absent; you stopped *trying*. I need you to hear why that matters."

She drags her attention back to me, and I wish she didn't. The pain in her eyes cuts deep. I want to bring her into my arms and hold her. I want to make her feel better. How can I be that man for her when I'm the reason she's crying in the first place?

"Work has consumed your time. At first, I overlooked it, thinking that surely it'll calm down. But then you went back on your promises. If we had a date, you'd reschedule it if work called you. When I asked for your help with a video, you'd agree and then forget about it the next day. You didn't notice when I went away for day trips because you were rarely ever at the house.

"I needed you, Elias!" She screams, tears running down her cheeks. "I needed you, and you weren't there. You're never there!"

Her words press down on me like heavy weights. "I was working to provide us with the life you deserve, Catalina. Everything I do—everything that I ever do is for you. All my success in the firm has always been for you."

"I don't give a shit about your success, Elias! I needed *you*. Not your success. Not your money. Not the fancy gifts you bring. *You!*" Catalina shakes her head, her words echoing around us.

After a beat of silence, she says, "It's not that I don't care about your career. I do, and I'm so proud of everything you've accomplished. You worked your ass off to get to where you are now, and I know you did it to give me a better life. But . . ." More tears.

More reasons to hate myself. I missed the point completely. I was so blind to her needs for so long. She never asked for more things. She asked for me. My time. My attention. I brushed off the little moments because I was tired or stressed or just had one more email to send. I always had one more thing to do.

When all my wife truly needed was me.

Catalina takes a tentative step closer. "No life is better without you in it and present. I married you, Elias, not the job and money you'd have one day. You understand that, don't you? It's important to me you know this."

The space between us shrinks, not just in distance, but in everything unsaid. I can see the wall she's spent so long building around herself, brick by careful brick, beginning to come down.

This time, when I reach for her, she doesn't flinch or retreat.

My fingers wrap gently around her wrist, and I draw her toward me, slow and deliberate, until we're standing chest to chest. Her breath hitches as her eyes search mine, and for the first time in a long while, she doesn't look like she's trying to escape.

She looks up at me with pain etched into every line of her face, but beneath it something else flickers. It's a fragile thread of hope she hasn't quite let go of no matter how much she's tried.

I cling to that.

"I thought I was doing enough," I say softly. "Providing for you—for us. But somewhere along the way, I stopped being present. And I'm sorry." There was no excuse for it, but I can't go back and change the past.

I'm damn proud of my job and having my wife by my side through it all. I love most things about being a lawyer and owning my own law firm, but she's right. My job takes up a shit ton of time. And for what? What's the use of having all this fucking money if I don't use it to take Catalina on vacations and spoil my girl with dates?

"I need you present, Elias. I can't go through feeling so alone that I thrived on the attention I got from my videos when I truly wanted it from my husband. Please don't make me choose between loving you and my own happiness," she begs, biting her lower lip.

I lean down, pulled by an invisible thread, and brush my lips against hers. It's a soft, fleeting gesture, but I hear her breath hitch. How starved for attention have I left

Catalina that a simple brush of my lips causes her to melt in my arms?

"Your happiness is with me, cariño, and only ever with me." I've been so close to pushing her away, but that shit ends tonight. Call it a Christmas fucking miracle or whatever, but Catalina will never feel unloved again.

"And I've never fallen out of love with you. Never." My words come out harsher than I intend.

Catalina flushes. "You . . . saw my Live?" She sounds embarrassed.

"Yeah, baby, when you make that proclamation for the world to see, I see it." I back her up against the couch. She gasps as I take her neck in my hand, squeezing just enough to get her attention. "That was a naughty thing to do, princesa."

Catalina's face turns into a scowl. "I was pissed at you! You deserved that."

Perhaps I did. "That shit ends now, Catalina. I'm your husband, and you'll never doubt that again. Never run to the fucking mountains and leave me without my wife."

She opens her mouth to give me a bratty response, but I violently yank her forward until our lips clash. A needy moan leaves Catalina's lips as fists my shirt in her hands to steady herself. I breathe her in, cursing myself for denying us these moments for far too long.

That ends today.

My wife's going to be sick of me.

I reach down, grabbing each of her thighs, and lift her up. She squeals, wrapping her arms around my neck to secure herself. "Elias! I'm too heavy—"

"Don't you fucking dare tell me you're too heavy. You think I'm a weak man that can't pick up his wife? Can't move her around to fuck her any way I wish? I need to remind you who your husband is." As I speak, I carry Catalina toward the bedroom.

Slowly, her legs wrap around me, giving into my demands.

"Good girl," I purr.

"Elias," she moans, burying her face into my neck. "I'm still mad at you," she mumbles.

"I can work with that."

"I expect you to show me you've changed. Sorry won't cut it if you don't back it up with actions." She tries to act stern, but her breathy tone gives her away.

I've no doubt she means her words. I plan to show her I intend to change. But right now, I plan on fucking her.

When I get to the bedroom, I kick open the door and carry her to the king-sized wooden bed centered on the back wall. Several quilts and pillows adorn the mattress so when I toss Catalina on to it, she bounces once and giggles.

"What if I said I don't want to have sex with you?"

I stand above her, reaching for the buttons of my shirt. With quick, skilled fingers, I undo each button. "Because you're upset with me?" I ask and once my shirt is open, I shrug it off and let it fall to the floor.

I don't miss the way my wife licks her lips as she looks me over. "R-right."

I smirk. "I suppose I would have to stop." Though I have no intentions of stopping as I undo my jeans. Catalina squeezes her thighs together. Once I have my zipper undone, I grab her legs and pull her to the edge of the bed. "Are you going to stop me, cariño?"

I know the answer before she speaks. Her gaze goes down my chest to the obvious bulge in the front of my jeans before slowly meeting my gaze. "You haven't had sex with me in a long time. I thought . . ."

More reasons to hate my fucking ignorance. I lean down, drawing her in. "You thought what?"

She bites her lip, hesitating before answering. "I thought you didn't find me pretty anymore."

"And that's my deepest regret," I say, invading her space. "For you to think I'm not absolutely wild about you. That I don't think of your body and being inside you at all times of the day. That I don't jerk off in the shower at the thought of you."

Catalina gasps, pink lips parting. I want nothing more than to fill her pretty mouth full of my cock. Later.

"You do that?"

"Every fucking time I shower."

"Then why didn't you . . . I mean I was right there!" She pouts.

I don't have an answer. Maybe I didn't want to wake her up or didn't think of her as a quick fuck I could get myself off with. I wanted to take my time with her and not use her for my own selfish pleasure. But I know one thing for certain. It's never happening again.

"That changes now." I snake my hand under her shirt, giving her a moment to push my hand away. When she doesn't, I slide it up further until my hand cups her heavy breast. She lets out a soft moan, and it goes straight to my cock. But there's still too many barriers between us. I need her naked.

Now.

As if thinking the same thing, Catalina grabs the hem of her shirt and pulls it over her head, discarding it on the floor next to mine. She unhooks her bra, letting her large tits free.

I'm a man undone and on her again. Our lips collide in a battle for dominance. She eagerly submits to me, parting her lips to allow my tongue to explore. My hands trail down her curves, loving how soft she is underneath me. My wife is sin incarnate, and I'm all too eager to indulge in her pleasures.

I hate myself for waiting so long.

Grabbing the top of her leggings, I peel them down her body, leaving her in nothing but a black thong that hides her core from me. That won't do. With another tug, her thong comes off, joining the other articles of clothing on the floor. I pull away from her lips and she whimpers from the loss of contact.

Needy girl. But I'm just as needy.

I drink in every dip and curve of her body. My gaze reaches the apex of her thighs, but my wife has her legs pressed together. I grab her legs, spreading her so I can see everything. Her arousal hits me and I groan, taking her in. Her pretty pussy glistens with her arousal, begging to be stuffed and fucked.

"I don't have the words to tell you how much you mean to me or to apologize the way you deserve, but I can show you," I say.

"Then show me," she says breathlessly. "I want you naked, too, Elias."

I press a kiss to the inside of her thigh before pulling back. I kick off my shoes and let my jeans fall. My black boxers go next. I'm so fucking hard for her. My cock is throbbing with the need to be buried deep inside of her.

Hunger lingers in her eyes when she looks at me. She reaches out and wraps a hand around my dick. I hiss in a mixture of pain and pleasure.

"This is how you apologize, Elias. With this. All night," she purrs like the tease she is.

"Does my wife need my cock?"

"You know I do."

"Say it." I have no reason to tease her. I desperately want to be inside of her, yet I can't help myself.

"I want your cock, Elias."

"Good girl." Seeing her face flush makes me smirk. I lean down and capture her nipple in my mouth, teasing the bud with my tongue. My hand moves between her legs, finding the bundle of nerves waiting to be touched. The first touch of my thumb against her clit has Catalina gasping and nearly pressing her legs back together, but I press my free hand to her thigh, keeping her spread and in place for me.

"Mine," I growl around her nipple.

"Yours." Her voice is drunk with lust. I take the opportunity to pull back and take her other nipple into my mouth. She moans just as I press the pad of my thumb down against her clit, rubbing slow, torturous circles.

She moans my name.

Fuck, I miss hearing her whimper for me. I miss how she squirms underneath my touch as I control her body. I was a fool to deny us this pleasure.

"Elias, please . . ." she begs.

And because I'm a dick, I ask. "Please what, cariño?"

"I need you inside of me. Please."

I want to take my time with her and milk every orgasm I can before I take her. But I have the patience of a child waiting to open their Christmas presents. There will be time for that later. I have all night to show her how sorry I am. Right now, we both need this.

I gently pull Catalina to the edge of the bed, settling

myself between her parted thighs. Her wide eyes, shimmering with love and a flicker of desperation, find mine. She needs to feel something deeper. She's aching for connection, and I feel it in every breath she takes.

I cradle her face, my voice rough with emotion. "You don't know how much I fucking love you, princesa. My heart is yours. It's always been yours. It will only ever be yours."

"Elias," she says my name with reverence as if I'm worthy of her worship. If the last year has proven anything, I'm not. But I'm a selfish bastard and eat it up.

I line myself up and claim her lips again. With one thrust, I push into her. Her tight pussy squeezes my dick, and we moan in unison. It's the best damn feeling in the world. Nothing could ever compare. "Fuck, Catalina."

I'm reverted to the teenage boy I was when I fell in love with her. We had finally admitted we loved each other and had sex for the first time in the back seat of my car. All those emotions hit me, just as they did back then. The love I have for her burns brighter than anything else in this world.

Her tight channel squeezes me in a way that makes me see stars. I'm not going to last long, but neither is she. We move as one, connecting in a way we haven't in a long time. Far longer than I ever intended.

I work my hips, thrusting in and out until we are both panting. Catalina digs her nails into my back, creating an intoxicating mixture of pain and pleasure. The only sounds in the room are our ragged breaths and the raw, rhythmic slap of skin on skin as we lose ourselves in the frenzy, desperate for release.

"I'm close. Elias, baby!" She gasps as I reach between our connected bodies and play with her clit. It's the last thing my wife needs before she screams my name, coming for my cock. I follow shortly after, my vision exploding with bright lights as I come deep inside her. Something primal in me loves marking Catalina, filling her up with my seed, and claiming her.

We stay there, panting and looking at each other. A soft, almost shy smile pulls at her lips as she reaches up to cup my face. "Love me forever, Elias. Not just today."

"There's not been a day since you came into my life that I have not loved you. You stole my heart, and I've never asked for it back. It's yours, cariño, always yours."

Until my final breath, I will love Catalina. Even when we're nothing more than echoes carried by the wind, my heart will still be hers.

And I show her repeatedly just how much I need and ache for her. I pour it all into every touch, every kiss, every whispered word against her skin. We move together long into the night, until her body trembles with exhaustion, and she finally surrenders to sleep in my arms.

Right where she's always belonged.

And when I'm certain she won't wake up, I grab my phone and prepare her final surprise.

CHAPTER 10

THE GREATEST GIFT

Catalina

I wake to the sensation of Elias nestled between my thighs and his warm breath ghosting over my skin. The scrape of his stubble sends a shiver through me, and I groan, instinctively trying to squeeze my legs together. But all that does is trap him more.

With a low chuckle, Elias tightens his grip and gently pries my knees apart. He looks up at me through the thick sweep of his lashes, a wicked grin playing on his lips. "Good morning, mi amor."

I don't get to return the greeting before his tongue licks up my seam, drawing out a loud moan. He's always had a wicked tongue and knows exactly how to make me squirm. This man has gone down on me for long periods of times, even when I beg for mercy. I miss that. But maybe we are getting back to the place we once were. Yesterday gave me hope and a newfound need to fight for our relationship.

Elias's tongue finds my clit. The first brush has me arching off the bed, reaching down to pull on his hair. He groans, and his hands grip me tighter.

"Fuck . . . G-good morning," I stammer, barely able to form cohesive words.

It earns a chuckle, sending shivers down my spine. If this is how he plans on waking me up every day, I think I'll be one happy girl. Honestly, every woman should wake up to a mind-blowing orgasm. We deserve it.

This man starts to eat me out in earnest. Each lick and swipe of his tongue has me rolling my hips, reaching down, and pulling his face closer to my pussy. I have never been self-conscious with Elias in my personal business. Not once in our relationship has he ever made me feel insecure or anything less than sexy. So, if he suffocates between my thighs, it's his fault for making me feel so secure.

I doubt he'd complain.

"Elias!" His name rolls off my tongue as pleasure rips through my body. His tongue teases my clit while he presses his finger deep inside of me, curling it slightly. "Fuck!" I gasp.

"That's it, cariño. Rub that pretty cunt all over my face. This pussy is mine."

Fuck, this man has a filthy mouth.

The sensation of his tongue and finger fucking me is too much. I'm still sore from the marathon of sex we had last night when he drew orgasm after orgasm until I went limp in his arms. I didn't think I would have another one in me so soon.

But once again, Elias surprises me.

He takes my clit into my mouth and thrusts a second

finger in me. I scream, pleasure erupting in my body like a white-hot charge that sends shockwaves. My thighs tremble as I come on his tongue, and he laps up my desire. Greedy man takes everything I give him, reminding me who I belong to. Who *he* belongs to.

My body goes limp on the bed, spent from orgasms I haven't had in so long. My vibrator can only do so much, but it's never made me come as many times as Elias has. Now I think I'm officially out of commission for at least a day.

"You insatiable man, go away," I giggle, trying to push him away from my very used and happy pussy.

He takes his sweet time pulling back, dragging his tongue slowly across his lips to savor the taste of me. The sight alone makes my breath hitch.

"Merry Christmas, Catalina," he murmurs, his voice thick with heat as he prowls up my body. His mouth finds mine in a kiss that's deep and unashamed. His tongue slips past my lips so I can taste myself on him. It's filthy. It's intimate. And it turns me on more than it should. He lingers, kissing me like he owns the moment—slow, possessive, and unwilling to let go.

Then his words register.

Christmas.

Holy shit, it's Christmas! Well, Christmas Eve. We've always exchanged gifts on Christmas Eve and gathered with family and friends for delicious meals on Christmas.

I break the kiss, eyes wide. "It's Christmas!" I repeat, earning a chuckle from Elias. He tries to kiss me again, but I swat him away. "No, you don't understand. It's Christmas, and I left all your gifts at home. Fuck!"

To be fair, I hadn't expected to leave my husband so

close to Christmas, and I certainly didn't count on him coming up here to spend the holiday with me.

Another thought slams into me. "Shit—you should be at work," I blurt, suddenly remembering his packed schedule. I've seen his calendar; I know how busy he is, especially this time of year. Sure, we talked about him cutting back and being more present in our relationship, but I never expected that kind of change to happen overnight. It's a huge ask—restructuring his workload, shifting priorities. Just because it's the holidays doesn't mean the world stops needing lawyers. The law doesn't take time off, and neither do his clients.

Despite my reeling brain, Elias just laughs. I shoot him a glare because this isn't a laughing matter, but he ignores it. "You worry too much, mi amor. I can help you relax." He winks, pulling me closer.

"You've helped me *relax* enough," I remind. Even if my heart jumps at the idea of sex with Elias, my body screams for a break. I'm not certain I'll survive another orgasm. "Are you going home, then?" I ask. The thought of him leaving fills me with dread, but I know—or hope—that this will be temporary.

"No. I'm not leaving."

"But—"

"Catalina," Elias says, his deep voice rolling through me like a slow, delicious shiver. He sits up in bed, settling against the headboard with an easy, confident grace. His arm reaches out, and I don't hesitate as I let him guide me into his lap, curling against him like I belong there. Because I do. There's no place I feel safer than in his arms and no comfort like the warmth of his embrace. I didn't realize how much I missed it until now.

He holds me close, then leans in, his voice soft but

firm. "I need you to turn that brilliant brain of yours off," he murmurs, lips brushing my temple, "and let me give you your present."

"Okay," I whisper. "I can't give you yours until we're home."

He just shakes his head. "You've given me enough. And, admittedly, most of your gifts are also at home."

"Wait." I pull back, brow furrowing. "You got me gifts? I didn't see any from you under the tree."

"Because it wasn't time to open them yet. Have you been snooping, cariño?"

I shrug indignantly. "Maybe." I definitely did.

Again, he laughs. "Naughty girl. Seeing as you didn't find them, I hid them well." He pauses, his confident demeanor slips and something vulnerable crosses his features. "But I have something for you now. Something . . . I hope you see as me hearing you and putting us first."

My curiosity is piqued, but I stay silent as he reaches for his phone on the bedside table. The screen illuminates as he slides it open, tapping the screen. I can't see what he's doing, but after a few minutes, he hands it over to me with no words or instructions.

"You're giving me your phone?" I ask, confused. "Am I supposed to search through your phone or . . ."

"I want you to look at what I have pulled up," he says.

"Okay." Still uncertain, I glance down at the app Elias has pulled up. My brows knit in confusion. "You wanted me to see your calendar? But—" The words stall in my throat as my brain slowly catches up with what I'm looking at.

Elias's calendar.

Elias's *empty* calendar.

I blink, thinking maybe I've misread it. But no—the

next two weeks are completely clear. No meetings. No court appearances. No client calls.

I swipe forward into mid-January, half-expecting the chaos to return. It does, but only in small doses. A few meetings scattered here and there during the week, but not a single appointment on any Sunday. Just one or two marked on Saturdays every other week.

My chest tightens as a mix of shock and emotion swell in my throat.

He cleared it. He cleared his calendar for *me*.

I try to say something. Anything. But each time I open my mouth, only shocked gasps escape. Elias is patient, giving me time to take in what I'm seeing. I don't realize I'm crying until Elias brushes my cheek with his thumb, catching a wayward tear.

"I hope these are happy tears," he murmurs.

"You . . . you cleared your calendar," I whisper, still unsure if I'm seeing it correctly. Like at any moment, Elias will come clean and say that this is all an elaborate prank.

But he doesn't.

This is real.

"I did and not just for you. For us," he says and cups my face. I glance up and we lock eyes. The grave set of his features and the sharp focus in his eyes make my skin prickle. "When you said what you said on that live? Fuck, Catalina, it devastated me."

I try to hang my head in shame. "I'm sorry. I—"

"Don't apologize. That shit hurt, but I needed to hear it and know that I've been a shitty husband. Making you feel like I was falling out of love with you was never my intention. By working and thinking I was doing my job as your husband, I was actually just pushing you away. I was fucking losing you, and I didn't even know."

His hands on my cheeks stiffen as emotion consumes him. He looks tortured, like he's punishing himself for all the mistakes he's made. I hate seeing him like this. "You can't shoulder all the blame. I should have spoken to you before it got this far. I didn't understand your side of it."

"Don't."

I freeze. "Don't what?"

"Make excuses for me. You never had time to tell me because I wasn't around. I haven't been around in a long fucking time," he snarls, but his venom isn't geared toward me. His ire is with himself.

I lean closer, pressing my lips gently against his. When I pull back, I take his face in my hands. "Do you love me, Elias Ayala?"

"More than anything on this fucking earth."

I smile, another stubborn tear falling down my cheeks. "Then that's the best gift you've ever given me."

We'll face our share of hardships as we step into this new chapter of our marriage. It will take some time getting reacquainted with being in each other's lives, but I've never been one to back down from a challenge. And if everything we've been through has taught me anything, it's that Elias and I are stronger when we're together. We always have been and always will be.

I may not know what the future holds, but one thing is crystal clear.

I never want to spend another Christmas without him.

EPILOGUE – ONE YEAR LATER

Catalina

"Welcome back beautiful people and thanks for hanging with me. It's Christmas, so you know what that means," I pause for dramatic effect. After a beat, I throw my hands up, tossing the flour I've been holding to look like snow. "It's time to decorate some Christmas cookies!"

Santi gives me a thumbs up from the opposite end of the camera, encouraging me to continue. I dust my hands off on my Christmas apron and make sure the sexy Mrs. Claus dress I'm wearing is properly covering what it should cover. One wrong move and this video will end up on an entirely different site.

Next to me, Elias is half naked.

I'm nothing if not a girl's girl, and the girls went crazy after my first viral video of Elias at the beach over the summer. My man looked damn good soaking wet, shirtless, and with his swim trunks hanging precariously low on his hips, doing little to hide the indention of his dick. It was truly a sight to be seen . . . so I shared it with my millions of subscribers.

Elias is shirtless now, which is both delicious and distracting, wearing red Santa pants with white fuzz at the ankles and a matching red apron. Santi had been adamant Elias wouldn't agree to the costume, and honestly, I thought the same thing, but he shocked the hell out of us both when he put it on without complaint.

Now I'm wondering how I can get him out of it . . .

Focus, Catalina.

Elias must sense me staring because he turns his attention away from the snowman shaped cookie in his hand to see me ogling him. He smirks—cocky bastard—and quicker than I can follow, leans down and captures my lips in a way that has me wishing Santi wasn't here.

"Oh, we are definitely keeping that kiss in," I hear Santi murmur from behind the camera.

I blush, giggling as we break apart.

I'm so stupidly and annoyingly in love with my husband. Judging by the fondness in his expression, I know he feels the same, too.

"Should we do it now?" Elias asks, and my brain goes to a completely R-rated place.

"Do what?" I all but squeak, which just deepens his smirk.

"Frost the cookies. Unless you want me to frost something else."

"Elias!" I blush, burning red.

"We're keeping that in, too!" Santi snickers.

We're *definitely* not.

The viewers would eat it up, though. Over the past

year, Elias has willingly appeared in more of my videos and has become a fan favorite. I'm certain some of my followers like him more than me. My videos always seem to do better when we're together, especially when he flirts with me.

> MARKERBANDIT: "THEY ARE SO CUTE TOGETHER!"

> ZOOMIEGREMLIN: "DAMNNNN, CATALINA, GET IT, QUEEN! THAT MAN IS FINE."

> MOODYCUPCAKE23: "HOW DOES IT FEEL TO BE GOD'S FAVORITE?"

Honestly? Pretty damn good.

We frost the cookies as we tell my followers about our love story. It's being written every day. We're open and honest about our past struggles and the changes we both had to make over the last year to make our marriage strong. We talk about how Elias has continued to maintain a work-life balance, thanks to the help of his firm partner, César. Together, they've been in the process of hiring more lawyers at the firm to pass some of their clients on.

Which means Elias is here a lot and has become somewhat of my unofficial manager for social media. He helps with video ideas, keeps track of finances, answers emails regarding brand deals, and takes care of all the legal shit that I'm not good at. In truth, he had been appalled at how little I knew, so he took over all contracts, which I'm fine with because legal language is so foreign to me. It's hot when Elias tries to talk to me in legal jargon.

We end up eating more of the frosting than actually frosting the cookies, but Santi promised it still made a good video. He promises to edit today and post tonight before taking a two-week vacation with Noah—a vacation I won't be crashing this year.

When Santi leaves, Elias wraps his arms around my waist and pulls me close. "Does Mrs. Claus want her gifts now?"

"Depends. Do any of my gifts involve you?" I hum, walking my fingers up his chest, earning a growl. Heat rushes between my thighs.

"And you say I'm the insatiable one." He smirks, his hands moving down my back to cup my ass.

I shrug because there's no denying it. I basically go into heat each time we have a moment to ourselves.

"I can be your present later, but I want you to open what I got you first," he says.

"Fine, but only if you open yours."

We shake on it before hurrying off to get the presents we bought for one another. Mine are under the tree, but Elias hid his out of fear I'd try to open them if he put them under the tree. Probably. I love gifts, and I tend to be too impatient to wait on opening them.

Elias joins me in the living room carrying four beautifully wrapped gifts.

"You wrapped those yourself?" I ask, impressed.

"Watched your tutorial." He winks, which warms something deep in my heart. "Did pretty good, yeah?"

"They're beautiful."

Elias settles beside me on the couch, the twinkling lights from the Christmas tree casting a warm glow over us as we exchange gifts. My heart races with anticipation, but despite my excitement, I nudge his pile toward him, insisting he goes first. As much as I love getting gifts, I love giving them more.

He starts with the smaller box—his favorite cologne, the one he's been casually eyeing for months but never bought for himself. A pleased smile tugs at his lips as he sprays a bit on his wrist and inhales. Next, he unwraps the envelope with two tickets to an upcoming NFL game—his team, front-row seats. He laughs, the sound deep and surprised, as he leans over to kiss my cheek while whispering, "You're amazing."

But it's the last gift that really gets him.

He opens the sleek black envelope and pulls out the boudoir album I had secretly put together—a surprise I'd been both nervous and excited about. His eyes widen, a slow, wicked grin spreading across his face as he flips through the pages. He flips back and flips again. He lingers longer with each pass, tracing the edge of a photo like it might burn him.

Yeah . . . I'm pretty sure that one is his favorite.

Next is my turn. I unwrap the smallest box, opening a beautiful and delicate necklace with a heart shaped locket. Inside is a picture of us from high school and etched on the back is the date we started dating. "I can't believe you remember that!"

"It was the second-best day of my life. How could I not?" he replies.

"Only second?"

"Our wedding being the first."

I smile.

The next presents are new mics, tripods, and studio lights for my videos. Until about a year ago, I didn't think Elias gave a shit about my videos, especially after he called them silly. Turns out he's watched every one, and now he makes sure all my equipment is working and even started his own social media where all he does is repost my videos or posts pictures of me. He's terrible at it still, but I love him so much for trying.

When I reach for the last present, I hesitate. It's about

the size of a small laptop—flat and thin, maybe an inch thick. A vinyl album, maybe? Though that wouldn't make much sense because we don't own a record player.

I glance over at Elias, searching his face for a hint, but he gives nothing away. His expression is unreadable, calm, and patient.

Curiosity gets the better of me, and I finally tear into the wrapping.

Once the wrapping paper is off, I turn the gift over in my hand to see a calendar. There are slight imperfections —a crinkled edge, a spot on the left-hand corner, and a cracked spine.

"Did you get me a calendar from a thrift shop?" Confusion laces my tone.

Still, ever so patient, he laughs and shakes his head. "No, open it."

I do.

There's writing in January. A quick flip through shows writing on every page. I turn back to January and see something marked for the second week. "Cruise dates?" I ask.

Elias nods as if I should know what it means.

When I flip it to February, I see something spanning two weeks. "London? What is this?"

"This, cariño, is a calendar full of vacations. The ones I promised to take you on when we first started dating, but due to my demanding work schedule, we never went on," he explains.

My eyes widen, mouth falling open. "So . . . " I flip to March, April, and May to see vacations dispersed throughout. "Is this real?" I ask, still unable to believe what I'm seeing.

It's all written out with blue ink in Elias's handwriting.

"Very real. I figured you could start a series of vacation vlogs. Always filming in a new place each month. And you could—"

I kiss him, capturing his words before they can fully form. Emotion swells in my chest, too big to speak around. This gift is the sweetest thing he's ever given me. Not just because of the travel plans—though those are incredible. They represent time. Time together.

Exactly what I asked of him a year ago.

And since that day, he's shown up again and again. Even when it was hard. Even when it would've been easier to slip back into our old rhythms and excuses. He chose *us*, every single time.

That's the real gift.

"Merry Christmas, Elias," I murmur, voice thick with emotion.

"Merry Christmas, Catalina," he replies, pulling me into his lap.

And then the world fades until there's only us. Only him. For now, and every Christmas to come.

SNEAK PEAK AT WICKED VALENTINE

Valentine's Day is a time for chocolates, flowers, and love. Or, in Lety Zavala's case, unbridled rage.

After being burned by love one too many times, Lety discovers a new hobby to boost her self-confidence: Cam

Girling. While her days are filled fighting attraction she has for her playboy boss at the office, her nights are for putting on a show for viewers. But one of her subscribers won't stop messaging. It's almost as if he knows her identity, the one she's fought so hard to keep hidden...

César Estrada is a lover at heart. Desperate for a relationship, but unable to keep a steady girlfriend, he resorts to finding his pleasure on adult sites. But when he discovers by pure chance that his favorite cam girl bears a striking resemblance to his secretary, he's determined to explore more--and make Lety his.

But Lety's aversion to relationships, and her secret identity, present an unexpected challenge César never saw coming. He'll pull out every romantic stop in the book and do whatever it takes to pull his wicked Valentine.

Preorder your copy here.

ABOUT THE AUTHOR

Anastasia Dean is a pen name for Tati B. Alvarez. She lives in Austin, Texas, where she spends most days lost in her own head, creating stories. When she is not writing, you can find her vacationing at Disney World.